Lee Aucoin, *Creative Director*
Jamey Acosta, *Senior Editor*
Heidi Fiedler, *Editor*
Produced and designed by
Denise Ryan & Associates
Illustration © Katie Saunders
Rachelle Cracchiolo, *Publisher*

Teacher Created Materials
5301 Oceanus Drive
Huntington Beach, CA 92649-1030
http://www.tcmpub.com
Paperback: ISBN: 978-1-4333-5524-0
Library Binding: ISDN. 978-1-4807-1692-6
© 2014 Teacher Created Materials

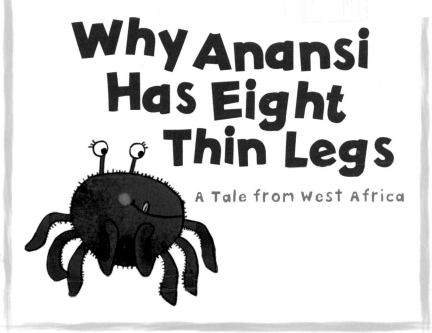

Why Anansi Has Eight Thin Legs

A Tale from West Africa

Written by Leah Osei

Illustrated by Katie Saunders

Once upon a time, a long time ago, there lived a spider called Anansi.

3

One day, on his way to the river, he stopped by Rabbit's house.

"Oh! You are cooking greens!" cried Anansi. "I love greens."

"They're not quite ready," said Rabbit. "But they will be soon. Why don't you stay and eat with me?"

7

"I'd love to, Rabbit, but I have some things to do," said Anansi.

He knew that if he stayed at Rabbit's house, Rabbit would give him chores.

9

"I know!" said Anansi. "I'll spin a web. Then, I'll tie a thread between my leg and your pot. When the greens are ready, tug on the thread. Then, I'll come running!"

Rabbit thought that was a very good idea, so that's what Anansi did.

As Anansi walked on, he sniffed the air.
"Mmm! I smell beans cooking."

"Come and eat the beans with me!"
cried Monkey. "They're almost ready."

13

"I'd love to Monkey, but I must go."
And again, Anansi suggested that he spin a
web and tie a thread to his leg and to the pot.

Monkey thought that was a great idea,
so that's what Anansi did.

15

By the time Anansi reached the river, he had a thread tied to each of his eight legs, for he had met six more friends who were cooking.

This was such a good idea, Anansi thought. *I wonder whose pot will be ready first.*

16

Just then, Anansi felt a tug on one of his legs. "Ah, that's the thread tied to Rabbit's greens," he said.

19

Then, he felt another tug. Then another.
Anansi was being pulled three ways at once!

"Oh, dear," said Anansi, as he felt a fourth thread pull. Then a fifth! And a sixth! A seventh thread pulled! And then an eighth!

"Oh my," sighed Anansi, as he rolled into the river to wash the threads away. "Maybe it was not a good idea after all."

And that is why to this day, Anansi the Spider has eight very thin legs.